GORILLAS' Night Out

Gorillas' Night Out

STORY BY **Faith Goldstein**

PICTURES BY **Elizabeth Brawley**

Gorillas' Night Out
Copyright © 2018 by Faith Goldstein

Indigo River Publishing
3 West Garden Street Ste. 352 M
Pensacola, FL 32502
www.indigoriverpublishing.com

Ordering Information:
Quantity sales: Special discounts are available on quantity purchases by corporations, associations, and others. For details, contact the publisher at the address above.

Orders by U.S. trade bookstores and wholesalers: Please contact the publisher at the address above.

Printed in the United States of America
Illustrator: Elizabeth Brawley
Editor: Regina Cornell
Book Design: mycustombookcover.com

Library of Congress Control Number: 2018964203
ISBN: 978-1-948080-60-6
First Edition

With Indigo River Publishing, you can always expect great books, strong voices, and meaningful messages. Most importantly, you'll always find ... words worth reading.

This book is dedicated to
Brandon, Max, and my entire tribe.

"If you can dream it, you can do it."
- Walt Disney

THE SUN began to set
and the sky turned DARK BLUE,

the CENTRAL PARK ZOO.

THE MOMENT the clock

started striking the EIGHT,

The **MISCHIEVOUS** monkeys...

...unlocked EVERY GATE.

Then, the animals would come out to PLAY,
singing and dancing
the whole night AWAY.

Yes, this happened EVERY night
at the zoo. It was a secret...

...ONLY the ANIMALS knew.

But...one night the gorillas
SNUCK OUT of the zoo...

Something they knew NEVER to do.

Tired of the same thing
NIGHT after NIGHT,

They wanted an adventure
SURE to EXCITE.

LEADING the troop was a GORILLA

named PETE, followed by friends

Skeet, Treat, and Little MARGUERITE.

13

They made their way down
to park avenue WEST,
Where stood the stores

of the VERY best DRESSED.

Pete led the way to the
FANCIEST STORE,
With luxurious clothing

from CEILING TO FLOOR.

They jumped on the COUCHES
and tried on the CLOTHES. They SWUNG
from the chandeliers by their TOES.

When they were DONE with all they
could DO, they left the store looking...

...for someplace NEW.

19

"Where to NEXT?"
the gorillas asked Pete.
"I don't know about you,

but I'm ready to EAT!"

All of their TUMMIES
were rumbling TOO,
So they found an ICE CREAM shop

on FIFTH AVENUE.

This old-fashioned shop sold
LOTS and LOTS of ice cream:
Cookie dough, rocky road,

and their favorite, BANANA SUPREME!

They SAT on the STOOLS
in this cute little shop,
And ate ALL the ice cream,

down to the very LAST DROP.

Strawberry   Mint Chip

Cookie Dough   Raspberry Tr

Rocky Road   Peanut Butter

27

Done with their ice cream,

it was time to see MORE.

The entire city was theirs to EXPLORE!

"Where to NEXT?"

asked Little Marguerite.

Across the street was a sign that READ,

"The SCHOOL for GYMNASTICS

and PHYSICAL ED."

The School for Gymnastics and Physical Ed.

They FOUND a big GYM
with equipment GALORE—
Ropes, rings, trampolines,

and a BOUNCY dance FLOOR.

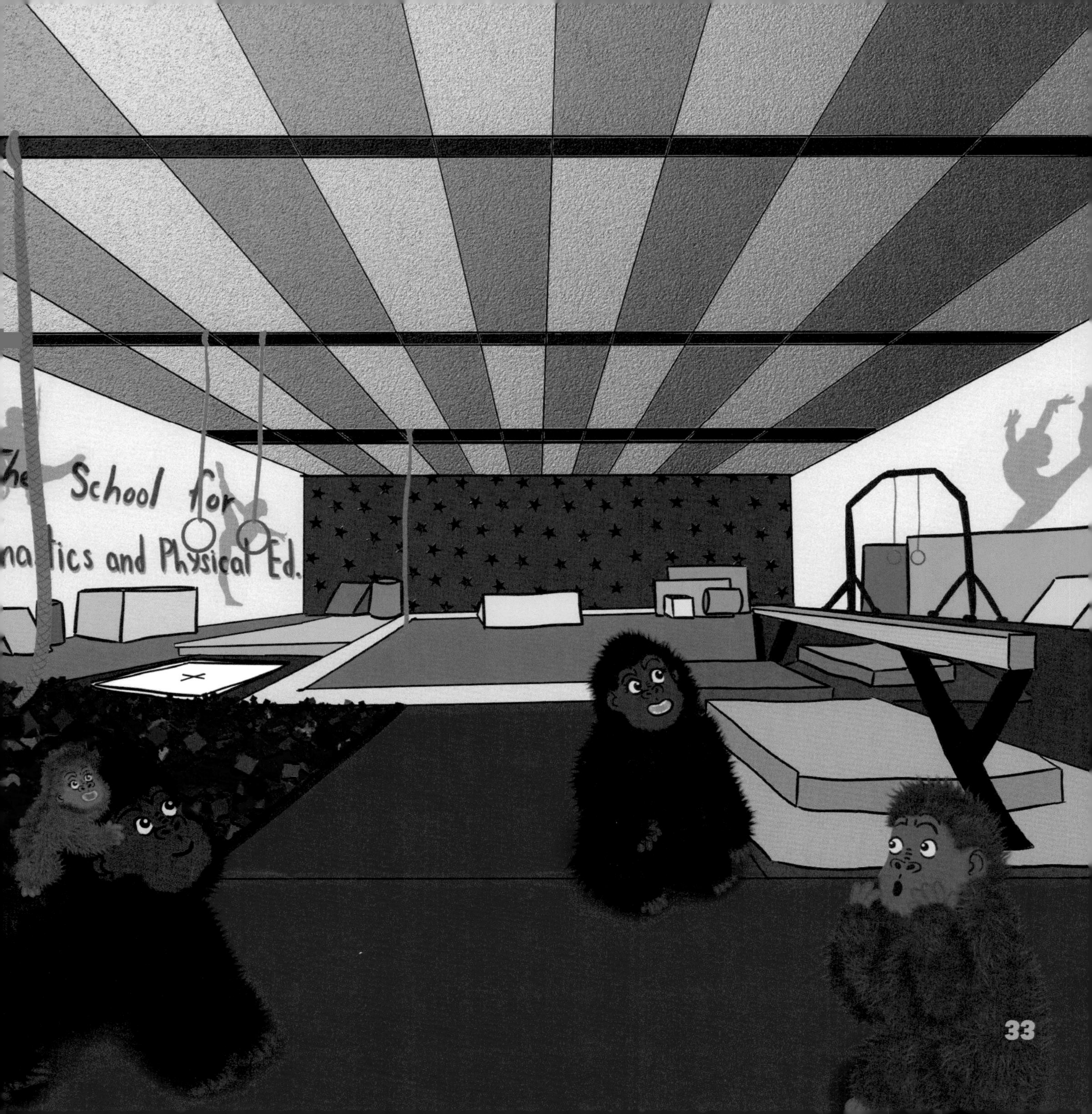
The School for
na tics and Physical Ed.

Pete DOVE into the cushy FOAM PIT,

While Skeet was on the beam

perfecting her SPLIT.

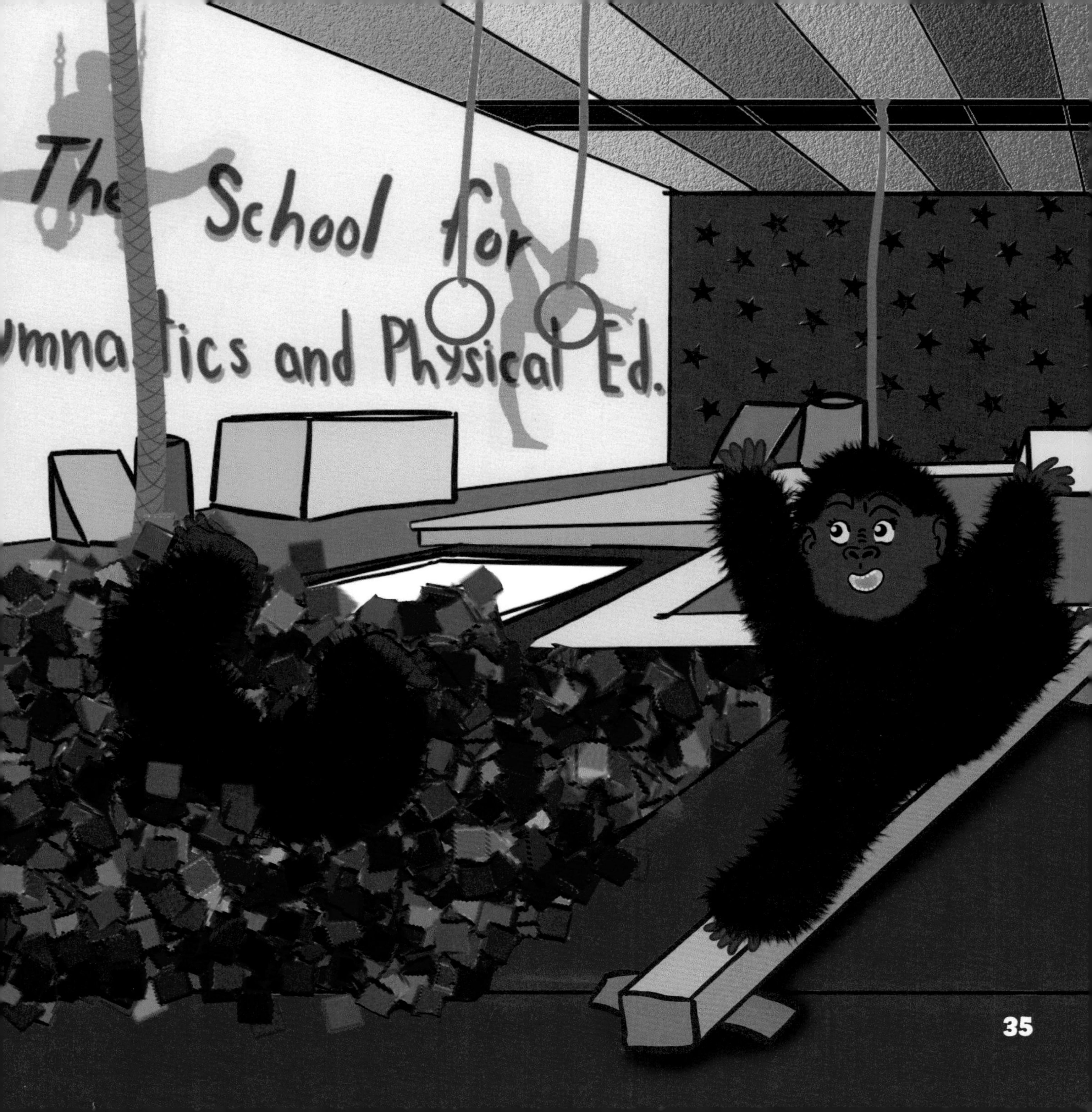
The School for
ymnastics and Physical Ed.

Treat did FLIPS and
SWUNG from the RINGS,
as Little Marguerite DANCED

in BUTTERFLY WINGS.

BUT...a watchman named JOE was making his ROUNDS. When he reached the gym,

he was ALARMED by ODD SOUNDS.

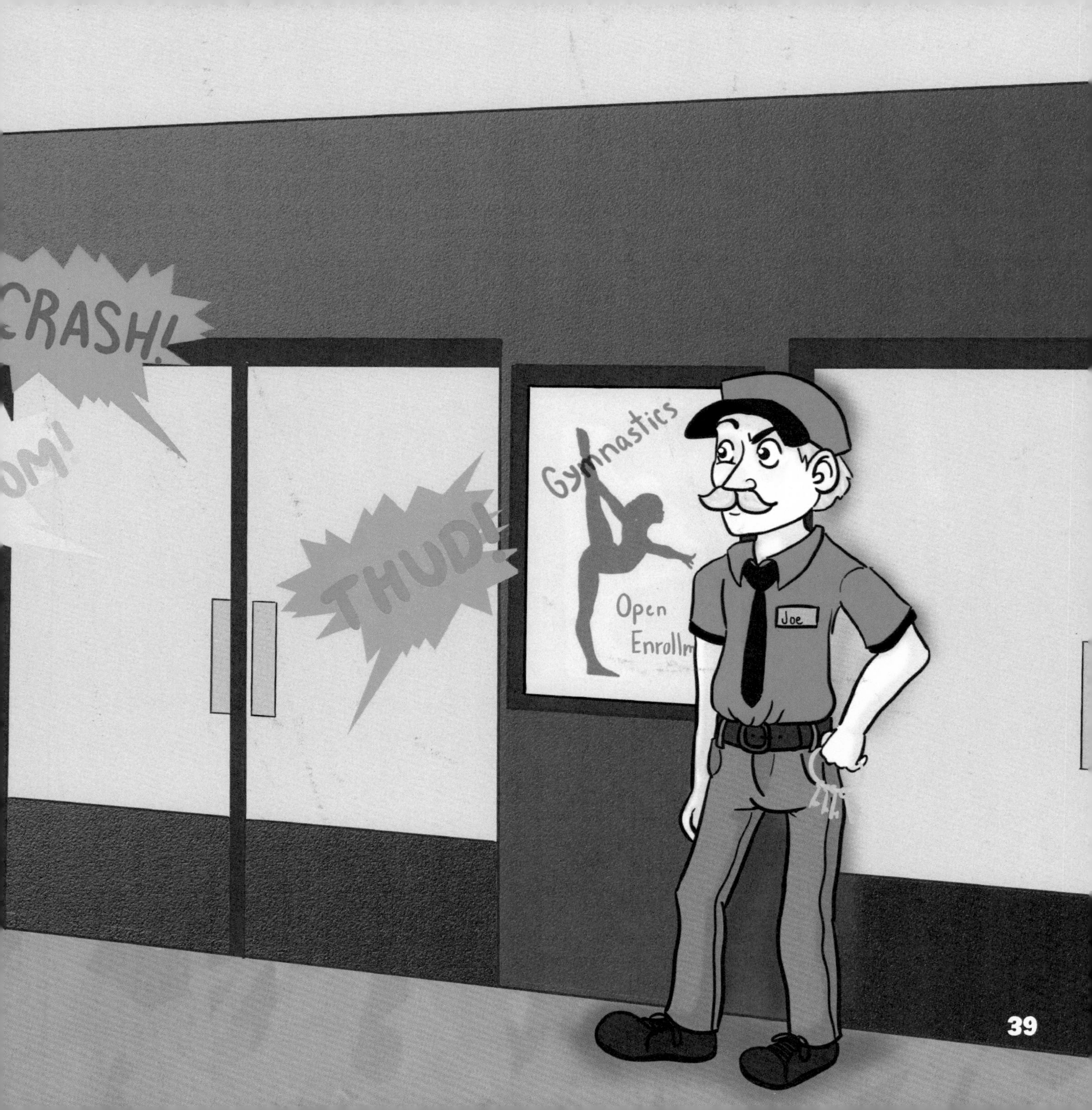
CRASH!
OM!
THUD!
Gymnastics
Open
Enrollm
Joe

Watchman Joe was SHOCKED

when he opened the door.

He saw the gorillas and fell to the floor!

"GORILLAS!" he shouted.

"They ESCAPED from the zoo!

Oh geez, gosh, golly,

WHAT should I DO?"

Pete cried, "GORILLAS,

it's time to be DONE!

Get READY, GET SET,

and now we must RUN!"

And run they did, like NEVER before,
all through the building
and out the front door.

Pete cried, "GORILLAS, I have a great
plan! Run back to the zoo...

47

Losing watchman Joe on Third Avenue,

They made it back SAFELY

to Central Park Zoo.

They CREPT to their cage
and climbed into their NEST,
Exhausted and ready

for quite a long rest.

The guests at the zoo

the very next DAY,

Were puzzled to see

the apes snoring AWAY.

The end.

Made in the USA
Lexington, KY
04 February 2019